CAROLINE LAMARCHE (Liège, 1955) is a novelist, poet, script writer and author of radio dramas. She studied Romance Studies at the University of Liège. Her debut novel *Le jour du chien* (Minuit, 1996) received the Prix Rossel. She is the author of eight books, including the collection of short stories *Nous sommes à la lisière* (Gallimard, 2019) which received the prestigious Prix Goncourt de la nouvelle.

KATHERINE GREGOR is a full-time literary translator from Italian and French. She translates fiction, non-fiction and plays. She was on the Premio Straga Jury in 2020. She also created 'The Italianist', a column about untranslated Italian books, for the European Literary Network. Her translation credits include Stefanis Auci's *The Florios of Sicily* (HarperVia), Marion Brunet's *Summer of Reckoning* (Bitter Lemon), Donato Carrisi's *Into the Labyrinth* (Little, Brown), and Sylvain Tesson's *Berenzina* (Europa Editions). She is currently writing a non-fiction book.

DR DOMINIQUE CARLINI-VERSINI is an Assistant Professor in French at Durham University in the UK and a specialist of contemporary French women's writing and filmmaking. Her first monograph *Le corps-frontière: figures de l'excès chez Marie Darrieussecq, Virginie Despentes and Marina de Van* will be published by Brill in 2023. She is also interested in inclusive pedagogy, translation studies, and feminist activism and thought, which she explores in her writing.

Caroline Lamarche

The Memory
of the Air

TRANSLATED FROM THE FRENCH
BY KATHERINE GREGOR

PRESS

First published in English in Great Britain in 2022 by
Héloïse Press Ltd
4 Pretoria Road
Canterbury CT1 1QL
www.heloisepress.com

First published under the original French language title *La mémoire de l'air* © 2014
Éditions GALLIMARD, Paris

This translation © Katherine Gregor 2022

Cover design by Laura Kloos
Copy-edited by David Watson
Text design and typesetting by Tetragon, London
Printed and bound in Great Britain by CPI Group (UK) Ltd, Croydon, CRO 4YY

This work has been translated with the support of a translation grant awarded
by Passa Porta and funded by the Service général des Lettres et du Livre of the
Wallonia-Brussels Federation

ISBN 978-1-7397515-2-4

Only a monologue can convey the truth –
who would dare divulge their secret to the other person?

ÜNICA ZURN

CONTENTS

Introduction

In her seminal feminist manifesto, *King Kong Theory* (2007), Virginie Despentes describes rape as 'a civil war, a political organization through which one gender declares to the other, I have complete power over you, I force you to feel inferior, guilty, and degraded'.[1] In the essay, Despentes draws on her own experience of rape when she was a teenage girl to reflect on its impact on women. She deplores the erasure of rape in women's writing, notably in French texts, and explains she found solace in American feminist writing when she was dealing with her own trauma:

> Prison, illness, abuse, drugs, abandonment, deportation: all traumas have their literature. But this crucial and fundamental trauma — the very definition of femininity, 'the body that can be taken by force and must remain defenseless' — was not part of literature. Not a single woman who has been through the process of rape has taken to words to craft a novel out of

9

her experience. No guide, no companionship. Rape
wasn't allowed into the symbolic realm.[2]

The textual erasure of rape Despentes refers to might
point to the ambiguous status of rape in French feminism.
Indeed, Kathryn Robson notes that rape has been a con-
tentious point amongst feminists of the second wave 'in
France and elsewhere. French feminist movements were
caught between defining women as, on the one hand,
self-determining individuals with bodily autonomy and,
on the other, (potential) victims of ever-threatening sexual
violence in need of legal protection'.[3] Although this ten-
sion divided second-wave feminist debates, the question of
rape is central to the twenty-first-century feminist agenda
according to Robson.[4]

Indeed, Despentes' assertion should be nuanced, as
women have repeatedly explored rape in their writing
since the 1990s. From supernatural tales such as Marie
Darrieussecq's *Truismes* (1996; English title: *Pig Tales*, 2005),
to more realistic approaches such as Meryem Alaoui's *La
Vérité sort de la bouche du cheval* (2018; English title: *Straight
from the Horse's Mouth*, 2020), Nathacha Appanah's *Tropique
de la violence* (2017; English title: *Tropic of Violence*, 2020)
or Virginie Lou's *Eloge de la lumière au temps des dinosaures*
(2001), rape can be considered a topos in contemporary
women writing in French. Many women writers have also
chosen to share their personal experience of sexual abuse in
their writing, most notably in Christine Angot's *L'Inceste*
(1999; English title: *Incest*, 2017) — or her most recent

exploration of the topic in *Le Voyage dans l'Est* (2021) — as well as of Samira Bellil's *Dans l'enfer des tournantes* (2002; English title: *To Hell and Back*, 2008) and Vanessa Springora's *Le Consentement* (2020; English title: *Consent*, 2021). As I argued elsewhere, rape is omnipresent in Despentes' non-fictional and fictional writing too.[5] Francophone women writers have also written about rape after someone else experienced it. For instance, in *La Robe blanche* (2018; English title: *The White Dress*, 2020), Nathalie Léger narrates the story of Italian artist Pippa Bacca, who was raped and murdered during an art performance in Istanbul. Similarly, in *La Familia grande* (2021; English title: *The Familia Grande*, 2022), Camille Kouchner tells the story of the incest her twin brother suffered. These multiple accounts of rape from fictional narrators, actual victims or witnesses highlight the frequency – even the banality – of rape in women's lives, but they also reveal the multiplicity of women's experiences of rape whether they are fictional characters or not. Thus, these literary explorations are a way to problematize the binary opposition that divided the second-wave feminist movement and that still structure some normative assumptions on gender violence. Indeed, these texts show that women can be both victims and active agents in control of their stories, consenting and raped, bearing witness and silenced at the same time.

Recently, the #MeToo movement has represented a transnational liberation of women's words outside of the literary text. It showed the world that victims of sexual harassment and abuse could take back control of their own narratives, creating new models of agency for women. Although initiated in Hollywood, it encouraged women as well as gay men from different places and industries all over the world to share their experience of sexual violence. It contributed to the emergence of new forms of feminist online activism and care networks. At the same time, it gave more women the strength to put their stories in writing. In the French context, this is true of two texts I already mentioned, Springora's *Consent* and Kouchner's *The Familia Grande*.

In turn, literary texts can have the power to bring about positive change. Indeed, in her self-narrative *Consent*, Springora describes her sexual and romantic relationship with fifty-year-old Gabriel Matzneff when she was fourteen. The relationship took place during the 1980s in France, at a time when the rhetoric of sexual freedom inspired by May '68 and the following years was still pervasive in the artistic world. Springora notes that their relationship and the many others Matzneff had with other teenage girls and boys were well known in Parisian literary circles and regularly featured in his books. After the publication of Springora's book in the post-#MeToo era, there was a widespread outcry and condemnation of Matzneff in the French and the international media alike. Matzneff lost a grant which he was still receiving from the Centre National Du Livre, a government body, and he has been shunned in literary circles. Some people who helped and protected him had to resign, notably Christophe Girard, who was in charge of culture in the Paris City Hall at the time. Most importantly, the text contributed to a broader discussion on consent in France, as observed by Elsa Court:

> Three weeks after the publication of *Le Consentement* (*Consent*), a group of 30 representatives in the Assemblée nationale introduced a proposal for the age of consent be set at 15, citing Springora's book: 'How is it possible to acknowledge having been abused,' reads the passage quoted in the proposal, 'when it's impossible to deny having consented, having felt desire, for the very adult who was so eager to take advantage of you?'[6]

Under French law the act of not saying no was understood as consenting (reminding us of the saying 'qui ne dit mot consent', in other words silence means consent), and the presumption of consent prevailed, even for an under-aged victim. Springora's text and the discussion that followed its publication in the French Parliament led to a change in the law, which now recognizes the age of fifteen as the official age under which a person cannot be considered to be consenting. Additionally, another victim of Matzneff's, British journalist Francesca Gee, recently announced that she will be self-publishing her own account of the abuse she experienced at the hands of Matzneff. Gee submitted her manuscript to Vanessa Springora's publisher in 2004, but she was told at the time that people were not ready to hear her story. Thus, Springora's narrative of sexual and psychological abuse led to the empowerment of women collectively and individually.

2. *THE MEMORY OF THE AIR*:
FROM THE INTIMATE TO THE UNIVERSAL

Reading Caroline Lamarche's *The Memory of the Air*, which was initially published in 2014, in the pre-#MeToo era, is a fascinating experience, as Lamarche's original text prefigured the movement, while the English edition, published in the post-#MeToo era, revives it.[7] The narrative is an oneiric exploration of the various forms of violence exerted on women through a subtle portrayal of domestic abuse and rape. Indeed, in *The Memory of the Air*, rape haunts the narrator, but its description only appears late in the text. The haunting is evoked poetically in the form of a dream that the narrator keeps having, the depiction of which opens the text:

> Last night I dreamt that, risking my life, I went down into a ravine and, at the bottom, found a dead woman. She was lying in a shroud, on a carpet of fallen leaves. I lifted the white sheet and saw her face, her closed eyes. She had rosy cheeks, a beautiful complexion, and didn't look her age, which—of that I was certain—was the same as mine: I hope I die before I become old.[8]

The first-person monologue uncovers the victim part of the self, as the reader gradually understands who the dead woman is. Like many texts dealing with gender violence, it is based on the writer's experience. Caroline Lamarche evoked the personal dimension of the narrative, describing the text as: 'a universal story, a sort of exemplary story and yet it's mine'.[9] Indeed, various textual strategies contribute to confer a universal dimension to Lamarche's words. The use of the first person and the anonymity of the narrator are ways to immerse the reader in the story as well as to foster a sense of proximity between narrator and reader. In addition, the restrained and elliptical quality of Lamarche's writing, which only reveals fractions of the narrator's story, actively engages the reader in uncovering it, and in that way, makes her or him a part of the story.

The universal appeal of the text can also be read in its political engagement. Although the text is neither militant nor overtly political, it displays a will to 'donne[r] la parole à une narratrice qui tente d'échapper aux codes sociaux régissant l'amour, la violence conjugale et le viol' ('give a voice to a narrator who is trying to escape the social codes governing love, domestic violence and rape', my translation).[10] The text subtly addresses the question of the victimisation of women who have experienced rape. Through the process of anamnesis, it deals with the guilt that the narrator has repressed, a guilt she is made to feel by male protagonists. Firstly, Manfore, the man with whom she was in a toxic relationship for several years. Lamarche speaks of 'a war between sexes' to describe their relationship, which is both passionate and psychologically and physically violent.[11] Manfore frequently engages in gaslighting and, on one such occasion, attempts to justify his own brutality by accusing her of being violent to him because she has been raped: 'You were raped a few years ago, weren't you? [...] You've never processed that rape, that's why you see violence everywhere, when you're the one who's violent because of that unprocessed rape.'[12] The narrator is similarly shamed by the police for potentially experiencing pleasure when she was raped when she goes to them for assistance. As police officers take her statement, one of them asks her whether she had an orgasm on the pretext that 'We need to know for the investigation.'[13] The confusion of her reply 'Yes-no-I-don't-know'[14] is met by an intimation to be silent about it, or to risk losing her trial, which plunges the narrator into anxiety as she imagines being questioned and challenged at the trial. By attempting to shame and silence the narrator, the police institution constitutes another form of control of the female body in the text. Albeit less brutal than the various forms of physical violence the narrator experiences, this institutional violence nevertheless leaves a mark on the narrator, and furthers her trauma.

3. ON THE IMPORTANCE OF TESTIMONY

In Lamarche's text, the narrator's attempt to tell her story to the police is perceived as a second violation, which mirrors many rape victims' experiences.[15] Zoe Brigley Thompson and Sorcha Gunne note that this risk exists in literary and other artistic representations of rape too, in which the rape can be appropriated as an object of consumption. At the same time, they emphasise the importance of literary and visual accounts of rape to subvert assumptions on sexual violence, adding that '[t]hese reconfigurations of rape narratives are important as feminism(s) attempts to move beyond the victim/perpetrator binary'.[16] Lamarche's text certainly offers such a reconfiguration. Through her writing, the narrator slowly discovers herself and finds a way to reconcile with the dead woman in the ravine. Although it is only alluded to, the reader witnesses the narrator's rejection of traditional gender roles and of heterosexual relationships. Hence, the story of rape and trauma is also one of finding freedom and self-healing through solitude. Lamarche sees her narrator as both 'solitaire et reliée. Elle est sortie d'histoires de couple qui l'assujettissent, elle est mue par une histoire qui est la sienne'[17] ('solitary and connected. She got herself out of relationships that subjugate her, she is moved by her own story', my translation). The semi-autobiographical dimension of the narrative means that this healing process is also Lamarche's, who claims that: 'Je ne me laisserai plus jamais dire que je suis inadequate lorsque je suis victime d'un abus de pouvoir'[18] ('Never again will I be told that I am inadequate when I am the victim of a power abuse', my translation). Indeed, *The Memory of the Air* is a striking testimony of the power of words and of their importance in our individual and collective understanding of, and dealing with, sexual violence. It is also a poetic encounter between the reader and a rich and complex female subjectivity. Today more than ever, voices such as Lamarche's narrator need to be heard, and Katherine Gregor's translation of *The Memory of the Air* is a timely contribution that brings this important voice into the Anglophone world.

DR DOMINIQUE CARLINI VERSINI
Durham University

NOTES

1   Virginie Despentes, *King Kong Theory*, trans. Stephanie Benson, The Feminist Press, 2010, p. 47.

2   Ibid., p. 38.

3   Kathryn Robson, 'The Subject of Rape: Feminist Discourses on Rape and Violability in Contemporary France', *French Cultural Studies*, 2015, vol. 26 (1), pp. 45–55, p. 45.

4   Ibid., p. 49.

5   Dominique Carlini Versini, '"Mais dégage"! Touch and Genderered Power Dynamics in Virginie Despentes's Novels', *Revue de fixxion française contemporaine*, 21, 2020, pp. 42–51.

6   Elsa Court, 'On the Limits of Sexual Freedom: Vanessa Springora's "Consent: A Memoir"', *LA Review of Books*, 17 February 2021 (lareviewofbooks.org).

7   The text was initially published by Gallimard in 2014 and is Lamarche's twelfth published work. Lamarche has published poems, novels and short stories and she was awarded the Prix Goncourt de la nouvelle for her short story collection *Nous sommes à la lisière* in 2019.

8   Caroline Lamarche, *The Memory of the Air*, trans. Katherine Gregor, Héloïse Press, 2022, p. 23.

9   Caroline Lamarche and Alain Veinstein, *Du jour au lendemain*, France Culture, 1 March 2014, https://www.franceculture.fr/emissions/du-jour-au-lendemain/caroline-lamarche.

10 Lori Saint-Martin, 'Plaisirs et dangers, aujourd'hui même : corps, codes de l'érotisme et contraintes chez Leïla Slimani, Caroline Lamarche et Nina Léger', *GRAATOn-Line*, 22 October 2019, pp. 33–56, p. 34.

11 'Guerre des sexes', Caroline Lamarche and Alain Veinstein, *Du jour au lendemain*.

12 Lamarche, *The Memory of the Air*, p. 78.

13 Ibid., p. 90.

14 Ibid., p. 90.

15 Zoe Brigley Thompson and Sorcha Gunne, 'Feminism without Borders: The Potentials and Pitfalls of Re-theorising Rape', in *Feminism, Literature and Rape Narratives: Violence and Violation*, eds. Brigley Thompson and Gunne, Routledge, 2010, pp. 1–22, p. 7.

16 Ibid., p. 4.

17 Caroline Lamarche and Alain Veinstein, *Du jour au lendemain*.

18 Ibid.

The Memory
of the Air

I

I

Last night I dreamt that, risking my life, I went down into a ravine and, at the bottom, found a dead woman. She was lying in a shroud, on a carpet of fallen leaves. I lifted the white sheet and saw her face, her closed eyes. She had rosy cheeks, a beautiful complexion, and didn't look her age, which —of that I was certain — was the same as mine: I hope I die before I become old. So, anyway, this dead woman was the same age as me, I'm sure of it, and yet she looked the way I did over twenty years ago, as though I myself had been asleep since then, as though I'd spent all that time dying. What happened twenty years ago, I cannot remember. In any case, although lifeless, the dead woman looked very much present, and alone out of necessity – the necessity of death. I promised I would ease her loneliness by paying her regular visits, thereby disregarding her true destination. Indeed – as is often the case in dreams – this was at once a live scene, so to speak, and a painting; and this work of art, this dead woman, was intended as a gift for the king of Nagorno-Karabakh on a festive occasion, the start of the literary season or something like that. But I'd decided not to add her to the other royal presents because, at least that's what I told myself, the king will receive many other gifts, so he won't notice the absence of the dead woman in the shroud.

I woke up determined to continue my conversation with the dead woman. When had she died? Why? Who had stopped her in mid-flight at an age when women are at their most beautiful? I had to go back and talk to her so that I could unravel this mystery. Would that mean having to go down into the ravine every time? It was a dangerous enterprise and a major one, but its reward, that sweet, peaceful face, that milk and rose complexion, those closed lids so wide they must conceal large eyes, eyes that see what people with open eyes can no longer see – all that gives me courage, as well as the desire, yes, to visit her on a regular basis.

2

Every morning, I think that everything is going to be all right. Or, on the contrary, that everything is going to go wrong. Either way, I have to go for it: put one foot in front of the other. Depending on the day, the descent into the ravine can be more or less easy. It's relatively straightforward to start with: the slope isn't steep and you start walking without a care in the world. It's later on that things become complicated, when your body gets tired and starts assuming slightly bow-legged positions owing to birth defects, gaps in your upbringing, or simply bad habits. Unless it's because of inadequately treated wounds – or wounds left totally untreated, like the ones that led this woman to her death.

When I woke up this morning, I had a few ideas on how to go down into the ravine without any mishaps. As soon I was up and had boiled the water for tea, everything receded: the ideal descent, the view, the landscape, everything I had outlined in the mist that comes before you get up. Moreover, I need to be clever enough not to wake anybody, and to reach the slope with my concentration intact, despite my life as an active woman. The dead woman is also alone, and nothing can mitigate her loneliness, which is much more drastic than mine, since mine comes and goes. Nobody makes her a cup of tea as I have just done for myself, nobody places a square of very dark chocolate – the kind I like – on her tongue, nobody looks out of the window to tell her what the weather's like, that it's grey, that it's chilly, that it's July – how I hate the summer holidays.

Yesterday, I fell asleep listening to a radio programme about borderline personality disorder. I've never thought of myself as being borderline and yet this morning – or perhaps even last night before falling asleep – I remembered that the last man I loved, *the man before*, as I call him (but before what?), said very early on in our relationship that he'd never met a woman whose moods changed so quickly, several times a day, an hour, or even a minute, and that it was a symptom – so he told me – of these people with borderline personality disorder.

What I'm wondering is: how come, with him, I displayed such a strangely mercurial personality and emotions, such extreme – *abnormal*, he called it – fluidity? How come it was like that with him and not with my husband, back in the old days when, on the contrary, I was always the same, always calm until our big annual argument, and how come things are different again now? Now everything is miraculously quiet, a bit like it is for the dead woman with the rosy complexion. She's like the Sleeping Beauty in our childhood books, who lay in a glass coffin, nothing touching her, nothing altering her.

To model yourself on someone else, to take on their colour or their illness, to live on the edge of yourself, always on quicksand. At school, they used to call me *the chameleon*. A compliment or an insult? *The man before* used to say, 'You don't know what you want.' Then he'd add, 'Just like my mother!' which would make me fly into a rage. When I was a child, I didn't like to be told 'You look so much like your mummy!' Is it possible to look both like a woman who doesn't know what she wants and another one who's inflexible? *Bringing up children is easy, you train them like dogs*: one of my mother's amusing sayings. Naturally, there are good owners, but also unpredictable ones. The dog then not only lives in fear of being beaten, but also of never knowing who it's dealing with, and ends up going mad. Is the owner happy or in a bad mood, and how does this depend on the dog? There's nothing like fear to make you attached to someone.

We had at least two things in common, *the man before* and I – three, if you count a love of books: we were great in bed, furious, tender, full of strange inventions, and that was the only thing that would get me away from my fear. The second thing was that we both lied to our mothers. Mine never asked anything. His would enquire, 'Don't you have a woman in your life, son?' and he would answer no. No, although he had introduced to her all the women in his life before me. No, although he made love to me every night whenever possible and got cross if ever I was too tired, like a little boy to whom you deny a toy.

But perhaps I'm going too fast here, perhaps I'm taking a wrong step by trying to summarise a seven-year borderline love like that. Perhaps I should go down a little more slowly, find a twisting path down to the bottom, where the dead woman is lying.

3

Dear dead woman, keep your eyes shut if you like, but make sure your ears are open: the man I loved for seven years didn't see fit to tell his mother I existed, that I was, as he said to me, *the love of his life*. And, for all those years, I didn't find it necessary to tell my mother that I would love him to my dying day. And yet my entire family ended up meeting this man, *the man before* – from now on, to make it easier, I'll call him *Man'fore,* Manfore. For example, how could I possibly abandon him on Christmas Eve? So I told my mother there was this friend who was on his own. Since Christmas is the season of goodwill, Manfore sat in the large dining room with us. He was astonished by the portraits of our forebears, by the silver hunting trophy on the marble sideboard, by my mother's impetuous welcome. 'Do you have any brothers or sisters? Are your parents still alive?' My father had just died: the end of an era. As for Manfore, he was inaugurating the age of experimentation. My longing for the impossible wore everybody out, especially me.

They say all love affairs are political. The way a hand touches your neck, your knee, your stomach, is political; the history that shaped this hand, the memory that makes it alive, its secret intention. Manfore's touch was heavy, the way you say a sleep is heavy when you can't tear yourself from it. Those hands possessed me, there's no other word for it, those hands that also wrote, but had equally gardened, cut wood and bent iron. In the past, he'd done everything with those hands I'd met too late. He kept saying that it was all pointless now, that he no longer had a taste for it, that he was bored, that his life had lost all meaning, except for writing and making love. I don't know if these two activities are connected to a point where they're interdependent. The time is increasingly distant when Manfore used to say to me, 'The only things that still work in me when nothing else does are writing and sex.' He seemed pleased with his assessment. But I was tired. Not tired of sex or writing, which offers so much surprise and variety. I usually don't get tired of anything. It's just that he shouldn't have repeated day after day that he'd ruined his life, that nothing would work out for him any more, he shouldn't have made me into a silent thing sitting on the sofa whenever I went to his place, a silent thing on whom he would spend a whole hour offloading everything that had gone wrong, was going wrong, would always go wrong, and then – once he'd done his clearing out, once I'd been filled and he was pleasantly empty – hope that I would be full of initiative and ready to form what he called *a normal couple* with him.

The sadness of men is a disease I catch easily, I'm not made of marble, or rubber, or soap, or cloud, their discouragement doesn't wash over me, it penetrates me, my skin is a sponge. Let me say at this stage that some people use me as a sounding board, as though I had no inner life whatsoever. They get upset at even the slightest reaction on my part, be it encouragement, advice or nervousness. They would rather I kept still and silent, like a dead woman smiling.

4

There is glorious sunshine this morning, so it's hard not to leap outside and take advantage, given that the weather forecast has announced a foul weekend. Still, I must first pay my little visit to the dead woman. She had a good night. She no longer minds the holidays. Yesterday, she went to the cinema, then had a beer in a café. Cafés are increasingly scarce around here, and so are good beers, but at least it's not a rough area, it's a part of our city where few people go, far from the street where Manfore lived and down which I no longer walk.

It's very pleasant just to let the holidays pass without leaving home. It allows me to visit the dead woman every morning. She and I have great conversations. For example, we draw up a list of things we no longer want. We no longer want to spend time with men who pretend to adore you but weigh a ton with their invincible defeat. For all its charm, we no longer want hysteria (and let me point out at this stage that it's not only the preserve of women). Basically, we no longer want a *normal couple*. Love for me, I tell her, is no longer a drug, no longer this hole you fall into, no longer wonder and terror, a relentless obsession, it's no longer one above all, but all above all. I feel sorry for couples I see in a tight embrace or constantly arguing, then inconsolable after a break-up, beaten, sublime, ridiculous: I, too, have been through this, I, too, have drained to the bottom the nectar that causes atrocious pain, I'm through with dying, being fluid, consumed to the marrow.

You're right, she replies, let's leave the consuming to flesh flies, known as *Sarcophaga carnaria*, who will do a very good job when the moment comes.

And yet, I add, there's something I miss that I'm forcing myself not to think about any more. To be honest, it's not life with a man. But *coming together* with him, in a bed that's not a bier, I mean, dear dead woman, a bed where one makes love.

And I describe to her how wonderful it is to sink with a man, travel with him a long way, all the way down, as far as what's called in French *la petite mort*, a little death I've always found to be very big, much bigger than the other one, which will sneak up one day and leave my body rigid. In this little death I float as though in very clear, very light water, the kind you find thousands of metres beneath the surface.

5

I sometimes think I recognise the dead woman. Isn't she who I was in Manfore's arms as he watched silently, after our *coming together*, my transformation into a smiling dead woman, eyes shut, gone someplace else, far away?

No.

Because the dead woman I'm talking about, whom I visit every morning, doesn't wonder day after day who's in front of her, what kind of mood he will reward her with, if she will have to moan or bite, or, on the contrary, get joyfully busy making sure he never lacks anything: a steaming plate in front of the TV, sexy lingerie for sex, and please wear your high-heeled boots, and put on make-up, I like that.

The dead woman I'm talking about is alone, relaxed like after lovemaking, she floats in this clear, light water, maybe having found her place at last.

6

To wake the dead woman, this morning I'm going to tell a brief story within the story. It's about our times and eternal childhood. In short, it's comprehensive enough for me not to comment about it further.

One day, I was in the city centre for some errand or other, no doubt necessary – otherwise why get stuck in this shopping thoroughfare lined with rows of chain stores selling clothes of local brands but actually manufactured in China, and Diet Coke-and-doughnut joints you find from Los Angeles to Kiev, by way of Brussels and Paris? In a draughty alley between two shopping centres, I noticed a boy of nine or ten, standing still in the crowd, holding little plastic men. His body language suggested that these figurines were being offered to passers-by for the benefit of a charity. He was a young volunteer, just as I had been at his age, recruited by the school or the parish: I had to walk up to people and, despite my pathological shyness, offer them my small item of humanitarian merchandise.

Seeing him, I didn't remember my terror back then, nor did I think about the man I'd just broken up with, the one I've called Manfore, who approached the world with huge reticence or didn't approach it at all, and waited for someone to look at him, basically to guess him, guess his great desire or his great fear of joining the family of men. All I saw was the strain in that face, still so young and so beautiful, and his anxiety increasing slowly, invisibly, paralysing him in the crowd. Only his outstretched hand and the little men told you why he was there. Otherwise, you would have thought he was lost or had been struck by lightning.

I smiled and spoke to him. I asked if he was selling actual *îles de paix* – it's what you call those little plastic men that look like stars. He said yes and his face lit up. I bought three. I didn't tell him he was very beautiful, I didn't want to frighten him. I told him he was brave, that he was doing something good, and wished him luck.

I left. But when I turned around I saw him, suddenly instilled with boldness, offering his star-shaped little men with an equally starry hand, his eyes flashing and his smile radiant and proud. Yes, he was zealously out to conquer passers-by, or rather one among them, the first who came along, who turned away, face inscrutable, shook his head and kept on walking.

When I think of Manfore, I do so in many ways. We had a complex relationship; a lifetime, or what's left of mine, wouldn't be enough to convey it. But on days of indulgence I think about him as I do about that little boy, his hand outstretched like a star, paralysed then radiant after a woman crossed his path. And I think of myself as that woman weary of the world and the bind of dealing with it, a woman who drew an innocent strength from that encounter.

As soon as we parted ways, I briefly looked back and saw how he came up against the crowd's indifference. Then I turned my back and went on my way. Now I wonder: what became of that little boy, did he manage to sell all his little men, and, if not, did he find someone to patiently put him back into the throng, his hands open like a star?

7

At the moment I'm reading a book called *The People of the Night*. It's not a novel, I prefer novels usually, but they no longer seem enough to help me go down into the ravine since I saw a dead woman there. It's a non-fiction work about miners, about the industrial revolution and the price men, women and children paid in order to tear from the soil the black gold that made other people rich. My family were part of these rich people. It's all been squandered since then, lost in the recession and the end of mining, of the *gueules noires* – men with blackened faces who were proud of endeavours now gone forever – a world my ancestors, hiding away in their houses for engineers, knew nothing about.

Manfore and I, our first meeting. A magazine editor gives us an assignment: to go to an old working-class district together. We're partnered for the purpose of the article, this bleak quarter will become ours, he will be your guide, I'm told. Never before have I set foot in that place deserted by my ancestors three or four generations ago.

Manfore's father, on the other hand, worked there shortly before his death. Every day he went to the factory, then all fire and smoke and molten steel, now a no-man's land behind a grey fence.

Manfore tells me about his father's and grandfather's work, about wire rod rolling mills, wire works, metal sheets, spools, wagons and barges with a sort of reticence, a melancholy laziness. I struggle in a tangle of omissions, not daring to ask questions, I look around for what he means, the stress of a repetitive, austere task, the noise of the machines, the silence of the men, their gestures unstoppable, their eyes glistening from blackened faces, but no, there's nothing left, even the dust doesn't rise any more, and I don't dare ask him to describe his father's and grandfather's bodies in motion, how did they move, what exactly were their jobs?

Every time we would argue over the following seven years, Manfore would throw my background in my face and curse his own. I would respond by saying nothing, guilty of my origins. Nothing would heal the feeling of the loss of a world, nor draw us close beyond it. The jobs of our fathers have disappeared and, with them, customs, anxieties, joys, ways to entertain yourself after work, of eating, drinking, dying. Relentlessly, without our even being aware of it, in our slightest gestures, the way our hands would rest, our bodies move against each other, the content of our quarrels, the flowers I would give him, a prisoner of my mother's habits, the bread he would eat slowly, like his father and his grandfather before him, the rice tart indifferent to class barriers, the staple snack of our childhoods, the books we care about, the words tossed out and the words unspoken, we would drill openings into the past, getting grazed as we went along. But, at this stage, when we first meet, in this ghostly region we have in common, it's still too little. For the sake of an article, we check each other cautiously, wrapped in consideration like the severely wounded are in cotton wool.

On this day I don't see the glory of my forefathers, I can't imagine their faces, their words when they forecast the future, bought, built, while the glimmering river carried their barges before their eyes. Since then, every last drop of the river has been polluted, and yet we can see two tiny fishermen on the opposite bank. What are they fishing? Dead fish, Manfore says. We gaze at the cloudy river, talk about the non-existent fish, the fishermen like something from a Beckett play, he says. We tread on oily gravel, find a blackened glove here and there, once worn by a worker, stiff, hand open wide, then another one, shrivelled and hard, and Manfore takes pictures of these lost or discarded gloves for the magazine.

In the only café on the main street, between two houses on which you can read *For sale* on one side and *No entry: health hazard* on the other, the manageress looks like a sur-vivor out of nowhere. Her perm dates back to the Stone Age, her printed T-shirt hugs her large, calm breasts, a panther roars on it, its maw blazing like the mouth of a blast furnace. On the walls hang amateur paintings: slag heaps, miners' cottages, a wood, a pond. We're the only customers, the billiard table has a protective cover on it, a slot machine is blinking for no one. I'm hungry. I think I see a forgotten bowl of peanuts on the billiard table. They're cat treats, Manfore remarks, and I suddenly recognise the pungent smell hovering in this café.

We go back out into the grey street, he walks in huge strides, as if trying to leave me behind, I follow him from a distance, astonished, embarrassed – am I supposed to run? – I skirt the fronts of other buildings, *For sale, This building is a health hazard, Clearance sale, For rent, After 120 years this company is closing down, For sale, For sale*, I trot after him, humiliated and confused. Later, on the slopes of a wooded slag heap where we lie down to enjoy a ray of sunshine, slabs of hard ice attract my attention. Strange: spring temperatures with these vestiges of ice in cracks in the ground. The sun never penetrates down there, Manfore says. His words make me feel that there is inside me a crack the sun never penetrates, a cold, frozen place of which I know nothing, not even what it's called.

8

And I'm at chapter eight already. There's nothing arbitrary about numbers. Besides, in numerology, according to the Web, otherwise known as the Internet, eight symbolises *the perpetual, alternating exchange of two polarities, be they androgynous or temporal*.

No one knows, probably not even me, if the story I'm telling concerns an *androgynous* entity – two beings inside me – or a *temporal* one – two beings who truly exist together at a moment in their lives. In any case, the Internet adds that *one is born of the other and* that *this requires going through essential stages*. How many chapters, hurdles, stages? My story will decide. Moreover, spiders have eight legs, we'll see if that isn't somehow connected to Manfore, of whom I speak not knowing if I'm inventing him or inventing myself.

What isn't invented is the spider I was watching spinning its web as I sat on the bench in the garden on the days when I was staying at his place. What happened to that bench I gave him, a good idea because that's where he'd smoke his evening cigarette, and I loved watching him smoke slowly and deeply, like everything else he did, in a silence barely disrupted by the song of a city blackbird? Of course I'm talking about summer, the season of the blackbird and the spider, which are both solitary and spin the thread of their song or web in order to mark their territory or trap prey. The memory of a childhood without television or videogames surfaces, the time of long, ever-so-long holidays and the tireless exploration of meadows. My little-girl's eyes were on a level with spider's webs glistening with dew or set by the first frost, like sugar lace. It seemed to me that the peace of the dawn depended on this persistent and patient task, a work of art as well as a trap, this way of crisscrossing the area, of catching whatever flies into it, stumbles across it, lands on it. The feeling of being in the centre, like the spider, is the same as when you're telling a story.

I knew this spider personally from having watched it in Manfore's garden. When he mentioned it that night, I said, 'It's a diadem — the most beautiful of spiders', to which he replied that there were other beautiful spiders in other latitudes. He said that knowing I wouldn't be able to help thinking about the women he'd sometimes hint at, the ones he had had, the ones he would still have, and the one he claimed he had on the days I wasn't there, no doubt an element, true or false, devised to keep me.

We were sitting on the bench. The weather was mild. Manfore lit a cigarette and pensively took a drag. He said, 'Did you know that spiders like cigarettes?' One of his tantalising questions, generally leading to a story. 'No,' I replied, laughing with anticipated pleasure.

43

Manfore then leaned towards the diadem spider I'd watched spinning its web for hours, at times looking busy, every so often stopping to test the resistance of the thread or else secreting a more abundant or finer one. And, instead of throwing his ash on the ground, he dropped it on the web. The spider rushed to the ash, turned it around in its legs and started eating it. He did it again and again until his cigarette was completely burnt away. The web also seemed to wear away, I thought I could hear a tiny sizzle, as all-consuming as my anxiety.

The night's chill made us go back inside. When we sat on the bench again the following day, all the ash was gone.

Having spun its web, the spider looks like it's resting. In actual fact, still at the heart of its trap, it's focusing on the capture. But now it will have to start by cleaning its hunting ground.

Night after night, eating ash.

9

I don't know what happened to the diadem spider. I hope I won't inspire any Machiavellian ideas by reporting this incident I found fascinating, just as I was fascinated back then by anything that suggested cruelty, the cruel game I was experiencing, which I no doubt fed on for some obscure reason I still haven't been able to identify. I remember that this fascination of mine stemmed from the notion of a game consubstantial with Manfore's slightest action towards me. Yes, we were playing an intense and extraordinarily complex match, like a game of chess in which it was I who was mainly led to being checkmated despite my queens, kings, bishops, and knights.

To be honest, I'd never learnt to play. Nobody played in my family. Neither draughts nor cards, nor dice, nor darts like in invitingly warm cafés. Our house had a silent library, with each one of us in their own corner, with their own book. Dialectics, diagonals, counter-moves, tactics, arithmetic were alien to the girls, who were educated to be naive; as for the men, captains of industry, they kept such things for stock market deals and their companies. Everything else was *Catholic*, a refuge from life's vicissitudes. We'd say of a person we didn't quite like or of a worrying situation: doesn't sound Catholic.

Blind faith wasn't for the coal miners: they were mostly Communists and ready to pounce on the priest; it was my ancestors who would pay for Mass to be said for the peace of their souls. I'd quite like to know if their souls were black or white, but their hands were certainly clean. As for the workers, after the mine pit, their charcoal-caked fingernails black with mourning, they would go to the garden to plant flowers for beauty's sake and vegetables to improve the humdrum. These allotments became known in French as *les jardins ouvriers*, workers' gardens. They also made room for music, which they'd play together, brass bands, open-air dances, while we listened to Mozart in a speechless sitting room.

As an adolescent, I wondered where babies came from and if I actually had two holes rather than just one in the front of my belly, I didn't know who Patti Smith was, May '68 was when my mother stocked up on sugar and my father brought a carved wooden blue tit from a trip to Sweden. At the same time, Manfore occupied factories and threw cobblestones, went to concerts by the Moody Blues and seduced, without doing anything, all the girls in our city who eventually made a mark on the world of culture and the arts. He even charmed the boys; his teachers called him *the Prince* and his friends *the best among us*, even though he'd once smashed the door to the principal's office by simply ramming his shoulder into it.

46

10

At this stage of my story, I hear echoes of my quiet life. My holidays in this city from which I don't stir. My daughters by the sea or in a holiday home in the mountains. I don't miss my mother – who's currently without me – and neither does she, but if we had to find a topic of conversation over the phone, I think, since she's always loved flowers, she would be interested by this piece of information: the flesh fly I mentioned earlier, *Sarcophaga carnaria*, doesn't, it seems, just devour flesh. It pollinates the goldenrod, a very resistant plant with a strong smell you're not sure whether you love or hate.

Even at a distance, it's comforting to feel surrounded by love when the moment comes to immerse myself in solitude. Because the time has come, I think, to undertake the tiny steps – nowhere near sufficient to cover the infinite subject of our meeting or the memories Manfore left to those who crossed his path – towards what will lead me to the crux of this story. In doing so I will gloss over some adorable episodes, everything that shows that, despite it all, we loved each other for a long time, and get down to the incident which split us up once and for all. As I write this, I know that Manfore could also write *I will gloss over some adorable episodes and get down to the incident which split us up once and for all*. Each will interpret this *incident* their own way, each will say exactly when it happened, the reason, the colour and possibly make him – or herself – look good in it. I could, of course, provide irrefutable evidence, but will only allude to it here. It matters little whether people believe me or not, it will be my word against his, the way it always is when there are no witnesses.

In any case, who's speaking? If you consider that every character you see in your dreams is a part of you, perhaps it's the dead woman speaking here. As for the place where she waits for me, that ravine with uneven slopes, it is as alien to me as Nagorny Karabakh.

I I

Nagorny Karabakh is a luxuriant but isolated enclave at the heart of the Caucasus, where one-fifth of the population died during the war of independence. A part of my soul, if the word still means anything, is also luxuriant, isolated, separatist. And if the war I've been waging ever since my childhood has burnt down a fifth of my territory all the way to my heart, I still have four fifths left. At the risk of instrumentalising the residents of Nagorny Karabakh, whom I salute from my personal little enclave, I observe that all individual struggles find an echo in those of nations, and that women who've been subjected to a totalitarian education since childhood often march at the head of protests. At this stage, I don't know the route of the protest, but I am determined to march until the dead woman wakes up.

12

So let's start. But where shall I start?

With the bedroom. His bedroom, which for a time was our bedroom. The room with the bed and the books. That room where he had slept with other women, more regular than I ever was, and where I only slept every now and then in order to keep him for ever (so I thought), or because I wasn't strong enough to spend night after night with any man – even though Manfore never was, for me or anyone else, just any man. Where I therefore only slept after we'd made love and after we'd been reading side by side for a long time. Where I had the cheek, something Manfore often rebuked me for, to sleep there with him only after such moments. And so it became the room of books and love-making. And of the bed. That bed where he would devour a novel page after page with quiet greed, then start telling its story out loud as though there was no one there and he was telling it to himself, for his own wonderment (except that I was there). Then he would return to silence and his reading, a block of quiet time for me, watching him as I lay on this bed that had become, through books and lovemaking, our bed.

He had put in this room two twin mirrors he'd made with his own hands out of carved door frames he'd cut out, sanded, painted and assembled. A big job, a job requiring strength and precision, calculation and imagination, in order to create from a heavy door these perfect, jet-black squares framing two tiny mirrors that reflected nothing. Not even the bed. Our bed.

But from this bed in which we slept, read, fucked angrily or gently, and slept again and again, from this bed I could see the two black-framed mirrors. Eerily small mirrors, too small for our great love and yet there they were, watching us relentlessly, facing us, like two security cameras. Two cameras that would have only filmed the movement of the air. That would have captured the slightest motion in the air whenever we turned the pages of a book or made what's called love. Two mirrors hanging too high up to witness anything apart from the air trapped in the room. As though these mirrors were a pair of blind eyes. Eyes that couldn't see what I was seeing. Something no one saw, no one knew, something I haven't told anyone. Or if I have, if I happened to say it in a moment of weakness, something no one believed.

He never opened the windows, always left the curtains closed. Against the light, I didn't notice their faded colour, the fabric that had turned grey. All I could see was what I called the whiteness of the curtains, their harmonious folds which from a distance made an impression I was quite happy with: I thought about the light behind them, that would one day stream in. And sometimes, secretly, at a certain time of day, when he went out shopping or to visit his mother, I opened the curtains, then the windows, and light and air streamed in.

By the window, there was a table and a vase with dried flowers. In front of this table stood a chair on which he would put his clothes at night then remove them again in the morning, immediately slip into them, getting dressed as soon as he bounced out of bed, even though he didn't bounce, even though he was slow, sometimes very slow, but always the first one up – surprisingly, really, since at the time he said his life had no purpose, which never ceased to amaze me given that I was there (my vanity, back then). Being the first one up, he would go and make the coffee and I could hear him doing so while I lingered in bed a little longer. All this was the setting of the most normal life of the lives I've experienced.

Until the day – or rather the evening, an evening when I was reading and he wasn't, or perhaps he was, I can't remember – an evening at the start of a night. He couldn't sleep, he was anxious, as he often was, angst-ridden, as he so often was. It was the period when he would repeat things like:

I'm finished
I've done nothing with my life
I'll never be anybody
I haven't written a book

I've written many books in secret
but not one of them will be read
nobody will ever read me
and yet I spent my life
my young life, my high life
my life with other women
my life working and hoping
spent my life dreaming of the moment
when my book would finally come to life
for other people besides myself
with the words of my book travelling across the world
like so many mirrors
for people who would read me
spent my life dreaming
dreaming about this book
and now I'm dreaming
about my death
because (he told me that night)
I'll end up killing myself.

I'll end up killing myself, this sentence subsequently returned about once a month, but I would hear it hissing in my head day after day and hour after hour or rather minute after minute and second after second and I'd try in different ways to fight off this sentence, which was maybe more than a sentence, which was – while waiting perhaps to be more than a sentence someday – a block of terror. Terror is blind, which I am not – and that might have been why he wanted me beside him all the time, not only while making love or reading. As if we could *see* the whole time. As if I was strong enough to *see* all the time, with no distraction or forgetting. As if I had to take the place of the two little mirrors.

In the end, I wouldn't say anything. I would resist, like the air. The air Manfore breathed. I would become the air that was constantly around him, the air that never left, the air that moved with him and grew still with him. *I'll end up killing myself.* Exactly how much does this sentence weigh on the air, how does it make it move or stand still, how does its repetition affect it, how is the air affected, day after day, hour after hour, minute after minute, second after second, by this sentence: *I'll end up killing myself?*

'When?' I'd sometimes ask. I'd throw the word *When?* into the air. And the two twin mirrors would reflect nothing, nothing except this motion of the *When?* in the air, between my lips and the mirrors.

'When?' I'd say, meaning *How long?* How long will we hold on with books and lovemaking? How long will books and lovemaking be stronger than this sentence: *One day I'll end up killing myself?*

But he would answer, 'When? I don't know. One day, when you're not here, when you've gone out, I'll end up killing myself.'

The air has absorbed this sentence. The air stores the memory of it. The memory of the air stores all our gestures, all our words, even the gestures and words we end up abandoning.

1 3

One day I'll end up killing myself. Several years later, I mean today, this sentence turned out to be an extra element in the nameless game Manfore played with me, and to which I have since given a few names. The game of the indefinitely foretold death, the game of scheduled disappearance, the game of my present terror and my solitude to come, the game of my present guilt and that to come.

And yet there were the books and our games on the bed, yes, it was the games and reading room, and our games and reading kept getting stronger, and that was the reason I stayed. Because to me Manfore, wanting to die and not dying because of books and his book dream, Manfore was, yes, literature. What I know about literature. From that moment on he had me in his grip, having chosen me for that reason at a time in his life when other women no longer had a place, I mean no longer the ordinary place, which they agree to occupy beyond games and books, which makes them stay there, playing the game of always staying at the man's side, even if they're dead, even if their intelligence is dead, even if their desire is dead, they stay there like little mothers.

A little mother. Something I obviously would have had to be, too. Never, alas, one as great as our respective mothers, never as brave, as well-organised, as lovable and loving as them. Our mothers, who also read, read relentlessly, like us. In my mother's case the Bible. In his, Delly.

Delly was the pen name of a woman who wrote in secret and became so successful that her brother joined her. From then on it was two of them, brother plus sister equals Delly. Delly's novels always have a Dark Handsome Stranger, a Persecuted Woman and Persecuting Woman, and it's all spelt out in revealing titles like:

Slave or Queen?
Painful Victory
The Lethal Rose
Gilded Misery
Laments in the Night (233 reprints!)
The King with Dreaming Eyes
The Devouring She-Wolf
The Walled-Up Maiden

I often wonder whether I haven't also been the Woman who persecuted and was persecuted by a Dark Handsome Stranger. Whether Manfore didn't, unconsciously of course, suggest this Delly-style game I agreed to play, the mental game of his mother and generations of trapped women. Whether the dark, lethally handsome child he undoubtedly was in his mother's eyes hadn't been loved exactly or almost exactly the way I loved him. And whether a mother doesn't trap you in that game for eternity when her son finds a woman to replay it with him.

Nothing, not even world literature, Flaubert, Kafka, Beckett, Faulkner, all those we loved, because of whom we made love again and again on the book bed, none of them was as strong as Delly or the Bible. Did his mother live through Delly's stories the way my mother did through the Bible? *By Him with Him and in Him / Honour and glory be Yours / for ever and ever*, that's what they stuffed my head with day after day since I was conceived, that's what I sought in love. As for Manfore, he was looking for a woman who would indefinitely agree to play the game of the Persecuting/ Persecuted Woman and the Handsome Dark Stranger. At last, he found me. Then lost me. And maybe he has since found one or two others who, like me, enjoy Delly-style games with no witnesses except two blind mirrors, in a secret that will always be well kept.

14

No one will ever know anything about the bed scene, about the performance we would stage on that bed. No one. About the scent I left there, about the time I spent watching him sleep, or about the place where he lay, outside my reach, his eyes closed, his hand abandoned, half open, about when it would clasp shut on me, my body taken, pinned down, pierced with adoration, anxiety, anger, and the twin mirrors watching us relentlessly, in their black frames that were infinitely larger than the mirrors themselves.

15

Here's a dream from all the dreams that came to me while I loved him:

A man is cutting my throat. I'm lying across his knees. His knife is notched, or perhaps it's the lid from a food tin, its edges jagged. He's smiling. I'm the woman lying across his knees, it's nighttime, and I'm the woman walking down the path and looking, it's nighttime there, too. I walk past and look at myself, I see the throat about to be cut, I see the body lying at an angle, I see my body lying across his. The path is where I take a stroll every day. It's dark now, the ruts are deep, the mud is streaming. I am on his knees, lit up, but only barely, by his smile, and I'm on the path, frugally lit up by the moon. In this dual, cold glow, I am surprised nobody is coming to stop this.

Somewhere else, the same man is building an animated model whose very precise mechanism drives awls into notches. Everything is working perfectly, with no bumps or interruptions. A meticulous little performance in perpetual motion before this man's eyes, his self-confident eyes. And yet I know how hard he's worked on creating this very charming contraption. I also know how long I've wandered before finding the path where the man I love is murdering me and where I'm begging him, and where he answers that he'll do it anyway.

16

Every morning, Manfore would get up before me, get dressed and make the coffee, which is surprising when you think that mornings, mornings in particular, had no meaning for him, but like fairy-tale heroes called on to fell an entire forest every day, he would get up at dawn to write.

Except for one morning – it was after a certain event, not the next day, no, a little later, my arm was still all bruised – one morning when he was fast asleep on his front, like a child, his stomach sometimes rumbling so cutely when he slept, and I was observing the mirrors glowing softly in the darkness.

Anyway, one morning when he was in a deep, mysterious slumber, I got up first, went to the bathroom, splashed myself with cold water and decided to go downstairs and make the coffee, as he did every day. A coffee I hoped would be as black as when he made it, as hot, as powerful.

No, I wouldn't manage it.

So I went back into the bedroom to see if by any chance he was waking up.

He was sleeping in a new position. I didn't notice it straight away because I was eager to huddle against him again, get inside him, so to speak. Despite my arm. Despite the bruise on my arm. Or perhaps because of the bruise. But after I'd got up he had turned onto his back, hands folded on his stomach, as if he was thinking with his eyes closed, or as if someone had laid him out with dignity on a bier.

I saw him dead.

In a flash, I assessed my loss with fascination, the void my life would be without him, the time I would have to kill working non-stop in a country far, far away and very, very cold, in order to forget the house where I'd stayed for such a long time, watching over him, so to speak.

What a handsome dead man you'd make (I told myself, seeing him), as handsome as in life, elegant, focused, calm even unto the grave.

It was a Thursday. Later that Thursday, at the time when, like every Thursday, he went out to see his mother, I left for ever the room with the two mirrors. I didn't want to come back someday and find him there, on our bed, after he had acted on a plan he'd been announcing day after day for seven years, and which I'd seen that very morning.

A very handsome dead man.

II

I

Like every year, I am once again in the clean, bare consulting room, with the screen, the examination table, the photograph of the stone goddess with multiple breasts spurting water, as many spurts as there are breasts. And the doctor, possibly the same one as last year, or a different one, they're all somewhat cold, all rather perfect, like institutional mothers whose family home is the hospital, that large home that takes everyone in, and so also me on this breast-screening day. Do I have breast cancer? Will I become a part of the statistics? I come here once a year to find out.

Lie down, lift your arms, the palpation, get back up, go next door, where an assistant who does nothing but that squeezes my breasts, one after the other, between two plates: my small, elusive breasts, crushed nonetheless, uneven, my not-quite-twin breasts Manfore loved so much, which fit entirely in his hand and which he would also palpate, in front of the television. I sometimes wished I could just fall asleep against him, in front of the television, without being constantly touched, sometimes it was the contrary, for some obscure reason he wouldn't touch me for ages. It was always all or nothing between us.

After the breast screening, the doctor said, 'You can get dressed again,' just before heading out of the consulting room. Where do all these doctors go when they disappear while you're getting dressed again, leaving you to exit on your own, find your way back on your own?

Before she went out, I told her about the bruise on my arm. 'I'd like to show it to you. I'd like a record. But I don't want to lodge a complaint, not at all.'

You don't lodge a complaint against the man you love. And even if I had stopped loving him, admitting that was possible, I wouldn't have done it: you don't lodge a complaint against a brittle man. From time immemorial exceptionally intelligent and sensitive people have been violent, that's normal, the drama of the gifted child, a book has almost certainly been written about this: a gifted child has too much strength for this cramped world, his very strength makes him suffer, no doubt this also happens to girls but differently, in a way that hasn't really been studied.

I was thinking all that without saying it, in front of the impassive doctor.

'Simply a record,' I said, looking at the mother-goddess with multiple, gushing breasts, the photograph I see year after year while the doctors change – this doctor wasn't the same one as last year, who wasn't the same one as the previous year's either: the hospital has as many doctors as the fertility goddess breasts.

I was ashamed to talk about my arm, I was almost certainly bothering her, I'd come for my breasts and here I was talking about this arm.

The doctor didn't flinch, her eyes still fixed on the prescription she was drafting quickly as she said, 'Go to A&E, it's in the basement.' At the hospital, bodies are cut up into specific areas that correspond to specific departments, floors, sections, corridors. 'They'll issue you a record at A&E.'

My arm wasn't an emergency, my arm was already an old bruise, blue veering on purple and green with a bit of yellow, as though studded with rust. No vitriol, no gash from a blade, no bottle smashed on the head, no kicks in the liver, no neck squeezed and so forth. In other words, I was far from dead. But as the calendar would have it, I happened to be there for my breast screening only a few days after the events. So might as well take advantage before the bruise vanished completely and I ended up believing that nothing had happened.

So I went down in the huge, silent lift, ding, ding, ding, three or four floors, I can't remember now. I don't know why the A&E department is always in the basement, perhaps it's a miniature hell. An accident happens so quickly, as does death (morgues are also in the basement), and yet you wait, you wait, you wait without an appointment on a chair among other chairs glued to the wall, all lined up, with people on them, languishing, injured.

I was sitting up straight and all. No emergency, no pain even. The pain was concealed under the sleeve, an old pain, even though it was only a few days old. I had in an envelope snapshots of my breasts, opaque snapshots that become discernible in the light.

The duty doctor arrived, a black man in a white coat. I wished he'd smiled at me instead of looking at me like that, after all I was smiling as I said shyly, 'I've come for a record of an act of violence against me.' I've always learnt to smile, you never ask for anything without a smile, and, actually, you ask for as little as possible, you mustn't bother people.

Whenever Manfore smiled, everything lit up. I adored his smile, so rare that it became as precious as a pink diamond, especially towards the end, because in the beginning a man is always cheerful with the woman he loves. In his case, 'cheerful' isn't the right word: he'd got into the habit of being sad long before I came along, so I'll say 'funny', full of entertaining ideas. One day, he slipped a note under his own door, on which he'd scrawled, with many deliberate mistakes: *hello, yor wyfe wolks around naked im front of the windos it has to stop*. It's true that there was no curtain on his bathroom window but you would have had to lean very far forward from the house next door to see me naked in the bath, but still, from his worried expression, I actually believed it, as if the neighbour's opinion mattered to him. Another day, he gave me a lovely birthday card on which he'd written: *Congratulations, thirty years from now you might have a quiet life with the man you love!* He was full of charm and seriousness. With him a smile was the reward for hours and hours of a dark mood, it was a victory I sometimes took credit for because, naked, I would almost always make him smile.

The black doctor at A&E didn't smile at all. I myself was quite tense but I was smiling because, after all, the events were a few days old and I was no longer in shock, I thought. I wanted a record in case I were to need it, a piece of paper I would put away at the bottom of a drawer in the hope that it would never come out of there, evidence, a memento, something to look at, read again when Manfore repeated, if I ever saw him again someday, that I had made it all up. I had already taken a picture, by myself, holding my digital camera with my right hand (it was my left arm). I had taken that picture just for me, so I would no longer feel as though I was mad after hearing him say that I'd been the one to raise my hand to him. I'd pointed out that he was a man, never mind a man, a human being twenty centimetres taller than me and weighing thirty or so kilos more, and that I was sometimes scared. To which he'd snapped back, 'You're the one who scares me, you're a terrorist, your violence is all the stronger because you conceal it carefully and trigger it in others.'

The black doctor gave me an odd look when I said I wanted a record of violence against me. Was he scared of me, too? Should I have sobbed so I'd look normal? He ushered me into a white room, left me there, disappeared. The room was practically empty, there was just an examination table and an armchair next to it for a relative or a spouse, an armchair that remained empty when I lay down. The kind of room where they isolate the homeless person with hypothermia or in an ethylic coma, a young man who's taken drugs or whose suicide failed, in other words those who've triggered the said emergency, not ordinary accidents.

There was an open French window that led to the outside, where it was cold and grey. I think it was November, I should know, I could check, there's a date on the record. Why wasn't this room heated? Why was the door wide open? Could I close it or not? Had someone been here before me who smelt very bad? Had someone vomited here? Anyway, was there a specific reason for airing this room to the point where the door had been left open to the cold, and me left there, in that cold?

I thought about how I was often cold at Manfore's. He heated the place very little, would tell me to close the doors properly, I'd forget, he'd repeat it patiently, or in a neutral tone, more often than not. Neutral was sometimes too much. Neutral made me feel as though I'd been slapped. Yes, I must have had a serious issue with violence. *Close-the-doors-will-you?* I heard throughout my entire childhood, *you're-getting-the-whole-house-cold*. I could have left, run away through this open door, walked, walked, until I found silence, the whiteness, the frost, the light gleaming on the snow.

The black doctor returned, a document in his hand, he closed the door then asked me to show him my arm, felt it, looked, felt it again with his cautious, neutral touch. On the document with the hospital letterhead, above his name and signed initials, he wrote: *a large bruise was observed on the left arm.*

I left with the document. I was as calm as when I'd arrived, and the doctor just as puzzled, nothing had changed, except for the French window, now shut. But the room had stored so much cold, so, so much cold.

I walked past the A&E bays: why hadn't they put me there, in the warmth, in a bay separated from the others by a simple curtain that allows communal heat to circulate and you to sense other bodies, other people, who've had some accident or other, sprained a foot while walking, pulped a knee at an energetic football match, cut a finger while slicing salami, an inexplicable stomach ache, the ordinary lot, normal life? Why not surrounded by people? Why that doctor alone with me, his neutral touch on my arm, in a cold room?

2

My arm is no longer in the first flush of youth, not as muscular as it once was. A few years from now it will be that of an old woman, and yet at this stage in my story it's marked with a very large bruise, like the ones children get when they fight.

We liked to fight. Manfore would pretend to punch me, he'd sometimes hit me on my breasts, in my stomach, next to my eye, I was afraid but he said he pulled his punches, 'I know my limits,' he said. I enjoyed it, that fear, the fear of a child playing wolf with their father or an uncle or an older brother, the fear of fairy tales and vast woods. At other times, he was gentle as a lamb. He went out less and less. Lately, he would say, 'I'm increasingly alone and that suits me fine.' Wandering through the house at night, writing, writing, writing, sleeping in the afternoon, repeating *I'm going to kill myself.* In return, I was *inadequate* (as he put it), and was so more and more, it seemed: from words of comfort to naive suggestions, inadequacy was becoming second nature to me.

That day, the day of the blow on my arm, I'm not sure what triggered the argument but I remember I was tired of his complaining, of his angst that was always greater than mine, of course (the drama of the gifted child). I can picture us: we were opposite each other, each in their armchair in the living room. I must have been *inadequate*, said the wrong thing. He pulled me back in line, he, the champion of the retort.

Now words, his words, my words were no longer sufficient in our arguments. Words are never sufficient, there comes a time when the body naturally takes over, so to speak. So I stood up abruptly, as though propelled by a spring, walked straight up to him as he was lecturing me, stood facing him, not touching him, though. I was incensed, as I was seldom incensed, 'I could kill you,' I said (one should never say entirely what one thinks).

In a flash he punched me in the arm, the one I'm talking about, the left one. I fell backwards, fell back down, yes, into the armchair opposite, he hurled himself on me, hit me in the stomach.

I bent my legs.

Let myself roll onto the floor.

Crawled to the kitchen.

He followed me.

On the floor, I was crying, repeating, 'Why are you doing this? Why are you doing this? Why ...?'

He stared at me.

He went back into the living room. He switched on the television.

I sat on a chair in the kitchen, rubbing my arm.

I was looking at the wilted bunch of flowers in the vase, the bunch I'd made, so rich in wild flowers that he'd taken a picture of it in a light that made the smallest petal sparkle. He liked to keep my bunches of flowers, wilted flowers that would become grey and dry, the memory of a summer at the coldest heart of winter. The photograph he took at the time when they were fresh would lie at the bottom of my souvenir drawer, a witness to these perfect moments, of pure joy, that happened between us: a simple bunch, a few flowers.

I looked at the wilted flowers. I took them and threw them into the bin. Then I carefully rinsed the vase, instead of, for instance, breaking it. As I washed the vase, I told myself: this time, I'm leaving once and for all. Then I thought of the picture Manfore had taken, of its light concealed in the souvenir drawer. I decided to stay.

In the living room, he seemed not to have moved, the television was still on, although the film had finished, or the match, I can't remember, it was that time of night when there's nothing interesting on any more, or else, on the contrary, experimental films.

As soon as he saw me, he stood up and said, 'I'm going to have my bath,' and went upstairs without waiting. He spent three quarters of an hour in the bath filled to the brim, no doubt reading an old book with concentration and passion, forgetting everything else.

That night, I decided we would talk about it the following day, about the blow to my arm I mean, not about the bath, where I also ended up spending a long time, while he was already asleep in the bedroom, me asleep in the bath until the water had turned cold.

Cold, cold, cold.

3

The following day, he said nothing had happened, that it had all been my fault, that I had started it, that it was I who'd raised my hand to him, that he'd been *afraid*.

'Afraid of me? You're so much bigger and stronger than me. Besides, I didn't even touch you!'

'Yes, but you were about to hit me!'

'I would never have dared,' I said.

'It's not the first time you've hit me!'

The only time I'd done it, I hadn't hit him, slight difference, I'd thrown a book at him. The book had flown in his direction and clipped his nose. His nose had bled slightly, notched by the edge of the book, a truly superficial wound: no trace left the following day. And yet Manfore had yelled, 'Looook what you've done to me!' And he'd hit me in my back, three hard blows, like at the theatre before the curtain goes up: *Pom, pom, pom!*

I have to, have to remember whenever I recall that I loved him, remember, yes, that theatrical *Looook what you've done to me!* and those three deliberate blows, *Pom, pom, pom!*

Pom, pom, pom! in my back, quite different from a book on the nose, a projectile with a graceful trajectory, its pages flying and the edge of one of them whipping a one-centimetre area, maybe less, of a man's large nose (if the bridge of the nose breaks, I believe it heals much more easily than a spine).

I quite like this book story: he being such a great reader, to throw a book at his head.

How he read! On the sofa, in bed, in the bath, focused to the extreme. He would look up only to tell me about the book as though talking to himself, for his own salvation or for the air around us, the air that keeps the memory of all the stories humans have been telling one another since the dawn of time.

Since the day of the thrown book and the *Pom, pom, pom!* in my back, I'd never again dared raise my hand to him, assuming that's the correct expression for throwing a book. And yet the day after the event, referring to the bruise that was turning black on my arm, he said, 'Yesterday, it was you who started it.'

Something started hissing in my head, I couldn't think straight any more, so I carried on saying, my voice weaker and weaker, that I expected him to apologise.

He didn't apologise. If he had, I wouldn't be telling this story now. He simply said, 'You were raped a few years ago, weren't you?'

You were raped. That was correct, an old rape. I'd only told him the bare minimum: I was alive even though the man had a knife. 'I've always been lucky,' I'd said to him back then, as though I wanted to offer a guarantee that all would be well between us.

Besides, it was a stranger, nothing to do with being struck by the person you love most in the world, who's the best suited to you in the world – in other words, the love of your life. It's easy to lodge a complaint when it's a stranger.

Complaint: I lodge a complaint against the stranger who raped me, a balaclava over his head and a knife in his hand.

Complaint qualified with the following: I'm alive. My family don't cast me out. I don't live in a country at war. Nobody inserted a branch or a broken bottle into my sex organ. I don't have AIDS. I'm not pregnant as a result of rape. I can even go back to a husband, if I want to.

That's what I told myself for many years. Until the moment Manfore said, 'You've never processed that rape, that's why you see violence everywhere, when you're the one who's violent because of that unprocessed rape.'

He was telling me, only a few hours after hitting me, that I was guilty of provoking his act. That I had basically asked, via the proxy of a lover, for the blow that was turning my arm black.

My eardrums started hissing, my brain seething, I could only think of one thing, which was strictly useless at that moment. I remembered what the police inspector recording my complaint had told me. He'd asked me a question that had plunged me into utter confusion. I replied – you must always reply to an inspector – something I might say some-day. He then told me I had to keep it quiet, that it would remain between him and me, because if I said it, it *would go against me in court.*

Would I be going to court?

I didn't understand.

It was the other man who was the criminal, wasn't it?

Or was it me?

4

It was a summer's day like any other. A truly cloudless sky and a dazzling sun. I'm deliberately using these clichés to indicate that it was very warm, so I was dressed quite lightly, in a bright-red dress, an unusual outfit for my usual hour-and-a-half stroll at least, but I was wearing my good trainers.

Do I feel like telling this? I don't know. But since a man once said to me that my violence undoubtedly stemmed from the fact that I hadn't come to terms with this old rape story, I am going to tell it.

As I do, I have no idea where this account will lead. I was talking about the knee-length dress, not at all a provocative dress, but – I admit it – red. I feel like saying that the trees were luscious, at the climax of their summer, like Manfore and I when we first met – we'd lived, as people put it. But I have no more desire to talk about him. If I have loved him, then it's over. The fact that he hit me is nothing. But that he should have blamed me for that blow on my arm because of my rape, that all suggests, and it's about time, that there should never again be a debate with such a false witness.

As for the rest, this rape is mine. Every rape, like every instance of giving birth, is unique and belongs only to the woman who lived through it. Not to the rapist or the doctor or the police inspector, or even to the husband or lover who are just characters in a story that isn't theirs, their importance measured purely by the words they've been given to say.

So I was walking down a narrow lane. To the left, a field where white cows were grazing, to the right a dense wood edged with brambles and nettles. I walked along this path at least once a week, it was a public park and there was seldom anyone in that spot, I was far from the entrance and the castle that's now a museum. A path for those who enjoy solitude.

I suddenly thought I saw a head pop out from the bramble bushes. Someone took a peek then quickly withdrew into the foliage. I nearly turned back but the apparition had been so brief it barely registered on my retina let alone my brain, which was taken over by vague thoughts and specific criteria: I had an hour and a half or so to go before the end of the school day, when I'd go and pick up my children, my two little girls.

I remember I didn't want to turn back over such a trifle, give up on the planned route, the loop, or, if this man was real, give him the impression I was afraid of him, I didn't want to offend him. Besides, had I definitely seen a head come out of the bushes? Perhaps I'd made it up. And if I hadn't made it up, the stranger must be far away by now. Someone who, like me, enjoyed secluded paths, in other words a fellow unusual walker.

He was, in fact, an unusual walker. Far from following his own route, as I was doing, since it was mine, it turned out that he had followed me, probably followed the red patch that was my dress from the park entrance. And that he was waiting for me at the precise spot where his head had popped out to gauge the distance and time left before I reached him.

Would I have been followed if, instead of a red dress, I had been wearing, for instance, a pair of shapeless grey trousers or if I'd been old, or if I'd been what I'd dreamt of being when I was a child – a boy? No doubt some will blame me for the red dress, if you follow the argument to its conclusion, assuming there is a conclusion in this kind of argument. Would I have been followed had I been dead?

But now I get to the truly crucial point of my story.

Like a jack-in-the-box, he suddenly pounced on me – the stranger from the bramble bushes, even more of a stranger since he was wearing a red balaclava. Red, I said red, just like my dress, with two holes for the eyes and one hole for the mouth.

There was a knife in his hand.

He grasped me around the chest. He was slightly shorter than me. It's true that I'm tall, and at that moment was still strong, at least inside my head. Because I exclaimed, as if in one of those children's games when I fought with my cousins, 'Playing cowboys and Indians?' Yes, that's exactly what I said, those very words. I remember that in May 68, when students were throwing Molotov cocktails in our street then setting up camp by the wall of the nearest high school, my mother, as she walked past them, her shopping basket filled with vegetables, would ask them, *Playing cowboys and Indians?*

There are circumstances where you can't laugh at everything, and certainly not at a masked stranger holding a knife. His response to my light-hearted teasing was to press the blade harder against my carotid artery and say in a voice that sounded hollow because of the red cloth balaclava, 'If you scream, I'll kill you!'

If you scream, I'll kill you! Suddenly, I didn't have my legs any more. Suddenly, he had to carry me, this man shorter than me but very, very strong, I could feel it, as he dragged me down the slope towards a ravine. During the descent, I became the sheep that suddenly realises that the abattoir is in sight: its legs fail it and – added complication – it has to be dragged.

I didn't have my legs any more.

We were treading on the previous autumn's dead leaves, over which more leaves, still green now, would soon fall from the trees I would never see turn red. My last summer, I thought, me, who'd always told myself that when I grew very old, I would ideally die at the end of the summer, in the light.

The light didn't penetrate the thick foliage of the trees, which were at the peak of their splendour. I could already see myself dead, my throat slit, beneath a carpet of leaves. I could picture my eldest daughter, then eight years old, escorted by police officers, I could picture her and her father, her father holding her by the hand, she'd be the first to glimpse a piece of red dress – *it's Mummy's dress!* – peering out of a mound of loose soil covered in displaced leaves, at first sight a place that would seem like the digging ground of a wild boar searching for old acorns from the previous season.

I pictured nothing except this scene as I let the stranger with the knife drag me to the ravine full of dead leaves. The ideal place: a layer of softness, dry that season, a secluded location, the kind of spot lovers are delighted to find after leaving the path and braving the thorn bushes (the effort was worthwhile).

And now

now

now

But to be honest it was nothing, nothing terrified me more than the knife still in his hand. Where would he stick the knife in me, afterwards –

Here again I must say, to my credit or discredit, as we'll see later, that I was capable of a certain presence of mind. I said to myself: what if I fake it? Women sometimes pretend to get it over with more quickly, to be rid of it. *You'll have to let him get on with it*, my mother taught me when I was fourteen, *never refuse your husband, but don't worry, it's only a brief moment of bother, and it's over pretty quickly after all.*

I'd never done that. Fake it. I'd never had to. No doubt I'd been lucky with my husband and then later I'd been even luckier with the one whose name I won't utter again.

Unless love is impossible for me if you actually fake it. But here, in this ravine full of fallen leaves, it wasn't a matter of love, clearly. How does one fake it? I wondered frantically, I was a novice in the field, my body had never lied.

No, it wasn't working ...

And apparently it wasn't working very well for the balaclava-wearing stranger either, still holding the knife, the knife he wasn't letting go of, and his terribly hairy legs (he'd pulled down his trousers): this is the memory I'm left with.

I had removed my panties without his help, if I may say so, and before that my red dress, regretfully but with no rush, I'd spread it carefully over the leaves, as things stood, might as well make our bed comfortable and possibly aesthetically pleasing, red blood on a red dress would be cinematic.

Yes, now that I think about it, I was acting level-headedly at the hour of my death. Because I had no doubt I would die in a few moments.

The knife!

And me telling myself: if he's mad, or if he simply loses control, what must I do so this knife spares me? Don't let him stick this knife into my sex, yes, I could already see the knife there.

Give him pleasure, that's the idea that came to me. Give him self-confidence. Let him find his currently somewhat failing manhood. So fake an orgasm. Let him realise his power, his success, even though for his part, well, he was struggling away inconclusively, still holding the knife, his trousers around his ankles.

No, it wasn't working, I couldn't do it, fake it, and it's that powerlessness as well as my terror of the knife that made me lose my head and weep and shout, 'Why are you doing this?'

Why are you doing this? Why are you doing this? Why …? I kept repeating it relentlessly, weeping, shouting.

Strangely, I was talking to him as though he was a brother, a cousin, a lover. Or a little boy you come across on the path, who's torturing an animal for no reason.

Why are you doing this? Why are you doing this? Why are you doing this? Why …

Suddenly, he got fed up, really fed up, with this question repeated, repeated and repeated while I was weeping and shouting! He abruptly stopped trying to do what wasn't working anyway, straightened up and said in a truly exasperated tone, 'Because I can't help myself!'

So here it is, the real answer: *Because I can't help myself!*

Poor loser, I thought, astounded.

I wasn't weeping, wasn't shouting any more. Poor loser. I almost felt sorry for him. I wasn't afraid any more, my mind was in control of the situation with this thought: Poor loser, poor *can't help himself!*

So here's the key, the reason for this masquerade, this game of cowboys and Indians, and for the sheep led to slaughter, and for the balaclava and the knife: *I can't help myself!*

He was putting himself back together, his trousers once more concealing his hairy legs and his sex organ, which I hadn't really seen, rather concerned, evidently, with the knife. He was becoming pathetic. Even so, he still had his hollow voice when he said, 'Get dressed!' I got dressed calmly. It was all over. It hadn't lasted long. Just a brief moment of bother, as my mother would say.

After I'd put my dress back on, red and creased, not even damp – at least I can't remember, I can't remember recovering my dignity, my joy, my red dress – when I got dressed and stood in front of him, wondering: what now? he said, 'Show me your ID card!'

'I don't take my wallet with me when I go for a walk,' I said shyly, though in fact triumphantly: I was alive, ID card or not.

The knife point had dipped at the end of a limp arm, but the voice was still acting authoritative, reprimanding me one final time in order not to lose face, that face still invisible under the mask. 'If you tell the police, I'll find you and kill you!'

'Yes, sure,' I said, happy and quite determined to tell the police, and as soon as possible at that. Other women mustn't be exposed to Mr *I can't help myself*, they had to be protected and my daughters had to be protected, my darling girls, who were waiting for me outside the school.

My daughters, my darling girls: I was going to run, run, run. I wouldn't even be late, in my only slightly creased dress, my red dress,

red,

red.

5

I still had time, that's right, I had time before school to go and lodge my complaint. 'Lodge' is what you say. I wanted to toss my complaint, slam it down, quickly, and have done with it! Something like: you can't let a lunatic with a knife run around freely, one who rapes women because *he can't help himself.*

At the desk, I said, 'It's about a complaint.'

'What sort of complaint?'

'A rape.'

The female officer called the inspector and the inspector dropped everything and let me into his office. In an earnest tone, he told the officer not to disturb us. Then he summoned three deputies, three well-built young men in their blue uniforms, with fewer epaulettes than him, the inspector, fewer stripes, fewer everything and especially fewer centimeters around the waist – the inspector was fat. One of the three had a gentle, serious look. I can't remember about the other two, one of them sat at a desk further back and put a sheet of paper into a typewriter, I heard the sound of the carriage and a clatter of keys.

The inspector looked like he was nearing retirement, he seemed like a kind, benevolent dad. He and I sat opposite each other, the desk between us. Around us, standing because they were subordinates, the two in uniform listened and watched while the third tapped on the keyboard.

I made my statement. I can't remember what I said. Do I have a copy of that complaint? Was I given a copy of that complaint? Back then I didn't keep my souvenirs in a secret drawer. I'm giving you all this from memory: the knife, the balaclava, the *modus operandi*. I said all that in a few words to the kind dad inspector, without looking at him, without looking at anyone. I was alive! alive! alive! After picturing myself completely dead. When that happens, you're not very chatty, or very sentimental. Strange as that might sound, I felt none of the six categories of emotions defined by Descartes, the philosopher, in his treatise *The Passions of the Soul*: Astonishment. Love. Hatred. Desire. Joy. Sadness. I no longer felt anything, I had suddenly turned into the coldest thing in the universe.

The inspector asked me a few questions, the size of the knife, for instance: a kitchen knife, a butcher's knife, a dagger? I didn't know. As far as I was concerned, it was a knife, its blade the length of a palm. I must have said something like that, apologising: 'I wasn't in the ideal position to assess the length of the knife.'

As I said that, I relived the blade on my neck, the blade in the hand close to my neck, the terror of the blade that might afterwards be stuck into my sex.

Maybe that's when he, the inspector – no doubt an intuitive man – felt that he could ask me the question that was really troubling him.

'Did you come?'

Had I heard right?

He repeated his question.

He added, 'We need to know for the investigation.'

Did you come? We need to know for the investigation. My mind was suddenly plunged into utter confusion, mush inside my head.

After a moment of silence – no one was stirring, the clicking of the typewriter had stopped – I replied exactly, that much I remember, I remember my answer perfectly: 'Yes-no-I-don't-know.' And that, very quick, of the inspector: 'Don't tell anyone else what you've just said to me, it could go against you in court!'

My ears were hissing, I couldn't think straight any more, I pictured myself standing opposite a large audience, someone at the bar saying, 'She came or faked it, she enjoyed it,' or worse, 'She fooled everybody.' All I could see around me, in this anticipated panic, were men in black gowns and white pleated neck doilies, ready to sentence me.

Around me, in the office of the inspector, fatherly and looking after my interests, there were also men. The clicking of the typewriter had stopped, undoubtedly there were things you shouldn't write down. So one of them had stopped typing. The other one, invisible, was saying nothing. And the third, the gentle one, the serious one, I sensed standing to my left, strapped into his uniform with no epaulettes or stripes, the nobody said, 'Chief, do we really all have to be here and listen to this?'

Had this sentence contained even an ounce of revulsion, it would have been for me the final blow, the sentence that kills. Tinged with nervousness, it would have offended a hostile inspector who makes and breaks careers. A sentence like that is made up of banal words, so banal they're transparent, everybody's words. After that, what's important is how the sentence is uttered.

Chief, do we really all have to be here and hear this? was said with such weariness and something so sad in his voice that I thought, I don't know why, that this nobody, this subordinate, had a beloved wife. Or a sister he loved. Or a mother who was still young, since he was also young. Or some close female friend or other to whom the same thing could happen as had happened to me. A man with respect and a certain amount of imagination, a man capable of putting himself in the place of a woman and from that place, thanks to a non-violent use of language, saying, quite simply, THAT'S ENOUGH!

Must the rest be told? Perhaps I'm too tired, or else in the state I was in for a few weeks after the rape. Nothing else could touch me, neither my children's smiles, nor their tears, nor their father's care, the way the memory of the man before no longer touches me.

They say that a body subjected to severe pain produces its own morphine. The mind, too, I think.

6

A few weeks later, I was walking down the street. I was thinking about nothing at all, or about unimportant things I had used to furnish my still confused mind since the rape. Suddenly, I saw a mother and her child, a little boy, probably at the 'no' age. His mother was shaking him violently, his mother was saying violent words to him, his mother was tired, exasperated, but there was nothing the child could do about it, I think, he was saying 'no' the way you breathe, the breathing of that tender age.

Besides, perhaps he wasn't even saying it, perhaps it was the mother's 'no' that was expressed in the child's tears, perhaps she was fed up with being a good mother, a good wife, a good employee or a good housewife, the good daughter of an elderly mother, perhaps she had an absent-minded, selfish, unfaithful husband, an obtuse or dangerous boss in love with her, perhaps it was all getting mixed up in her head, too.

I'm not judging.

I'm simply observing that the child was there in the wrong place and at the wrong time. A powerless being. A being over whom one has all the power.

The mother didn't slap him, didn't hit him on the arm or anywhere else. The mother shouted, cursed, while violently shaking the crying child.

At that moment, I understood what had happened to me.